*The city's streets are so wet s
Another car flies past. A rum
my ears and eats my mind. Th*

So this is where it all started. I suppose that it will end here too.

He is sitting motionless. A young man. Long hair. Anonymous.
Uninteresting. Average.

*So much aggression and frustration pressure rising up. In me?
Would I cry. I would. Turn up the volume, stand against the
intensity of the moment the music, shiver and cry.*

Tears are streaming down his face.

*This feels like, cold, desert sand tundra arctic storm blast
lashing my naked flesh. So cool over this heat.*

It has been so hot and humid outside recently.

*The rain storm leaves a freshness; the fleeing zephyrs of east
deliver brief respite. Cool is all I need. No more heat.*

He sits down and lights a joint, inhales, and whistles the hot
smoky air from his lungs.

The music in the room begins to swell louder and he lays down
on the sofa. He turns his head and looks out of the large window.

Grey streets and buildings.

The wet air, thin weak, the rain soaked windows, that thin trickle of condensation seeping down the wall, leaving line on the smooth satin paint. Filling me. Panicking me. Its fearful symmetry, its oneness of being, the beautiful clarity it afforded, its line straight.

The room fills with the choked stale smells of the street below.

This brand new brave new world, it can take you higher than the Milky Way, street life.

Dark grey wet tired street are falling asleep now. Grey buildings gaping windows for eyes staring down and out as the people make their way home from their dull office jobs to a warm home. Doors open mouths shut now.

Nice that. Going home to someone. Someone to welcome you in. Like a cat coming home after a night on the tiles. Lovely. Sky clearing at least. Rain has to stop. Still. First rain in four months. Been so hot.

Staring out across the asphalt of the roads, his eyes follow the path each car makes.

Look. Each drawing its line and its trajectory. Each tracing its future pattern and leaving its past in its wake. The tyres sucking up the rain and making a new dry pattern.

Fascinating. No really.

The lights on the rears of the cars flick on and off as the driver squeezes the brake pedal.

Harsh braking. Soft braking. Manic driving.

Sex and car crashes? Can't see the attraction in that at all. But then. Yeah I guess it's like when there's a documentary on about the death camps. Nazis. Secret experiments. Don't want to watch. Feel kind of dirty/wrong. But still can't shift the fascination. As long as it isn't children. Then its just sick, No stomach for that. But what man does to man and to woman. Depraved. But can't stop watching. Or finding out. Reading about it sometimes, stumble across that kind of thing. Eyes tend to stay on the page. Feels wrong but. But.

He looks left and right, peering out, sitting on the window ledge. A few people walking up the streets. An elderly couple struggling pulling their little trolley home between them.

Kind of smiling and laughing at something. Looking happy. Working together as a team.

A tramp walks not far behind them watching the floor and the gutter for dry patches. His beard and hair matted. He puts out a hand palm upwards and looks up. His coat is patched and worn. Trousers ragged at the bottom from years of dragging the grey streets of this town and the many many more he has walked.

Searching for something.

What are you looking for? What did you run away from? This? This loneliness you swapped somewhere for your new life out there? Is it still raining? Can't tell.

The tramp smiles a little, skips slightly and moves across the busy road, forcing drivers to stop and swear at him as he nips in and out between them, making his way towards the shelter offered by the war memorial.

Good hunting ground there. Been there many times meself. Picking up the old dog ends and twisting out the tobacco into a fresh skin to make a new fag. Heh.

Row on row of names. All dead. All gone in the Great War. Fathers, cousins, children, lovers. All in all millions of names across the world. Mostly young men. The women who die in wars don't get such grand memorials. They die vomiting and sick or mutilated and tortured. Unholy nasty killing.

I try to see clearly, to clear the fog from my eyes. I want to see.

He looks up as a spider scuttles across the ceiling. It had seven good legs, one was smashed and useless. It stopped briefly, snap, for an instance before casually passing the day, and leaving to squat in a corner of the room, by the door.

Out of view now.

Incinerate all the pigs, one by one. Flaming out of an ark everyone is a pig. Theyrall pigs. Hate you everyone. Fat pig priest butcher, sanctimonious smile flicks across the wet lips, glistering lips, a bead of sweat on his chin, spit. Hands rubbing - looking for sin. Cold hands woman's hands. The silver of rings. Ahh. An holy cross, beads all the signs and omens hung out before. That smile grew. Shifted across the holy face of greed ridden religion. It was twisted into a sneer. Lips moved but no sound come out. A silent movie. Almost black and white.

Almost funny. Almost.

Sometimes I sit and think I have seen the truth. Suddenly it all becomes clear, momentarily, I am at the complete loss of care, an instant of happiness. Cares gone. Vanished. All was. When my mind is blank it creeps up. The air splits. Bang. Wow. Crash. A tear. Rip. A gash in the fabric of a mirror, thousands of cracks. Hanging in the air - Revealing? A blurred view of an utopian paradise?

He lies on the fawn sofa the light across his face is unnatural now. the dull orange glow of the street light. The sky has darkened almost to a black now. The lamp so high outside shed little light on the street below. His body twitched and rolled over eyes bright and seeing.

Not surprised to see you there. Not shocked by my hallucinations. Not surprised by time travelers. You there from so far away in the future peering back at me myself here. Like two mirrors going into a feedback loop. A time-traveler? Or real. You decide.

Take you. Wherever you want to go, for I can teach you of heaven and hell. Messiah come to save your worthless souls. Heaven is so light it spins as it shines. Yet darkened it can be. The gods do not always shine.

He coughs and stands up and paces across to the window, picking up a packet of cheap French cigarettes on the way, lighting one.

I gaze without seeing, oblivious of the travelers below. Once a good game, working out what they thought, how they spoke. Who you are, and you, but now it's boring.

He picks up a pile of papers and smiles sideways leafing through and carefully studies the radio play as he closes one eye as the curling smoke from the cigarette makes it water. He smiles again looking up from the manuscript towards the open space outside.

Am I searching for my meaning in my own black words on white paper? Perhaps. Christian , his rhetoric slipped onto the carpet he thinks he's Christ.

He has a storm across his face now. Tears rolling down his young face , softly into his boys beard , drawing heavily on the cigarette clutched lipward . He puts the cigarette down briefly, resting it on the edge of the ashtray and sits on the windowledge. He is just gazing out. Eyes glassed over. Staring unseeing

He is thinking.

Who are you? Are you really me? Or a mirror of me? A fragment of time spun back here to now from then, the future?

He's slumped down now wiping his face with the back of his hand.

The sweet tears on my lips saltytaste tart bitter. I just sit and stare , I eat - I drink . God . I. Copulate with sterility . I am for you - am you , in all of you people , heh ? And we're all pigs ? Just as worthless just as stupid .

Prove me . Wrong me if you can . Test the untestable earthshattering faith of your mothers . Try to find in me your God . Can. Not. Be. Done. You will not burn as a pig when you die . I laugh as I watch you bleeding as you hang . I watch day turn to night as you cry as you suffer . I sneer . As you pray I sneer , at your fear . You bleed me like a wound . I gape . And the blood flows and yet you want more .

Screams filled the air. Splinters of bone. The sharp knife cuts the soft flesh. Screams and laughter. The wound gapes as I plunge in to the throbbing oozing flesh. The heat of her this was intense. We two are joined during dreams. We five or six people. The warmth of it floors us, we sigh. You and I as we make love. Corpses lifeless in memories past splendour. Oblivious of my caress screaming in your deaththroes - warm so soft heat.

I remember being given the ring. Its all a bit hazy. I don't need this now. Memory normally so sharp. Perhaps thats why I started drinking? Who can tell? Only a few now and again, nothing serious, just the joy of release. To forget, to be blinded, oblivious, obscenely pissed, laughing, and knowing that everything had gone for a time, a respite.

That night had been so dark and she was so beautiful, standing in the shadows, speaking so softly and gently. The gift was made in a blur of time. A distortion of reality.

*And then there is nothing. But the memories flood in and out.
Like waves on a beach.*

*What a time it was though. Drinking partying, talking till
daylight and living. Something I do so rarely now. Living. It was
all a whirr, a time of new interests, excitements and new
expectations. Driving through the dark looking for a party.
Trying speed and hash, making a path in life. Long hot summer
nights short in darkness days spent recovering, in the open air,
sitting in cafes talking and daydreaming about the future. There
was always somewhere to go. Something to do. Someone to talk
to.*

We could choose words like lies, as evening falls around us.

*I don't even remember giving that ring away. Or really what it
looked like. Celtic design? Pewter? Heavy. Or was it thin.
Feminine. So sad . The thoughts and feelings behind the giving
of that ring were so honest . An honesty I haven't had since . I
want to cry again. Cant.*

*She's gone now as if she had never existed. What was her name.
How did we meet? Where was it. She held me some times. Held
me close. Her warm flesh hot against me. Confusing me. Mixed
emotions. Ha! Not as much of a cliché as they say. Find clichés
be real. Sometimes. A friendship and a love so pure and
unrestricted a glowing love.*

The spider had settled itself into the corner and spun a small web. The streets were empty now and he looks like he has come down from the drugs that he has been taking. The only light in the room now , was from the small table lamp on top of the stereo .

He studies the spider, still smoking.

Certainly large, big for this time of year.

The spider remains motionless.

Still for fear of missing a catch. Asleep but seeing it all. Master of traps.

It was a time long since passed when freedom turns into captivity. Now I am old, twenty four. Even I can see the humour in that. Old. Twenty-four. What would it be like to be thirty? Now that really is old.

Music filled that earlier time. Bands. Gigs. The Black Lion. The Roadmender. So many blurred nights. Not blurred by drink but blurred by excitement. The thrill of it. A new life following the sterility of school. Another release. Set free from constriction. So much time space and freedom. So little to be responsible for. Responsibility?

He shrugged.

So much music burning at that time. So many long conversations. So much to be done, to look forward to, so many bright futures. So many bands seen, some good some bad, some indifferent but all trying. All doing. All making and creating. A bursting creativity surrounding this grey lifeless town. Not lifeless. All towns. Everytown. Everyone trapped but everyone free.

The Black Lion so many memories so much buzz. So many people and times and places again swim through him.

Good old Charlie. First time I had proper met him. First time sat there in that courtyard garden music drifting out to us. Spent most of our nights out there. Damn good times. Only place easy to get a drink underage. Black witches. Or was it red witches? Pernod, blackcurrant and cider in a half pint glass. Heheheh. Loved that place. Old bikers. Young punks. Skins sometimes. Usually all quite friendly. Bopping up and down to the local bands on the scene. Never really my thing or my sound. The Sound of Music. But still. Shrieking female singers. Gloomy techno vibes. Lots of rhythm and blues stuff. Oh and wonderful wonderful memories. Stolen kisses. Unexpected kisses and hand-holding. Being really alive not like dead now here feeling wounded lost cold alone. Experience beckoning. Pumping bass from funky bands.

That time we three or four punks sat at that metal gig watching the bikers fill the room. Watching uneasy. They passed around a brown paper bag. Assume it was brown? Passed it round. Vomiting in it. Why? Was it glue? And what was Charlie banging on about? Ahh that's it. Snipers on the rooftops. No real snipers. Was he so far out of it? Snipers and aeroplanes coming in to dive bomb us. Laughing deep real laughs. Talking and meeting. Listening and discussing. Interviews. The detritus of Northampton coming and going alongside the chosen few. The eliterati. Rubbing shoulders with so many of them. Dark smelly gloomy and certainly an unwashed and unloved place. Grimy mid-week sessions playing pool with the bikers out the back. Watching Slim the skinhead, his right hand on top of Jack's head as he pogoed up and down to some funky beat combo. Sizzling acoustic guitars humming and strumming. So many of them. So much time to kill. Good times. The bands all got up and did. They made those things, those events, that music. So much creativity. An explosion of sterile youth rising up.

Inhale. Exhale and breath deeply.

Yeah so thats what punk gave us. Three chords and a song. Shame. Missed punk properly first time round. Too young. Too young. Heheh when Egan came round that time and I was listening to The Stranglers and he was really surprised.

Nice middle-classed boy like me listening to that. Taped off the Top 20. Off the radio anyhow. Other gigs. Dancing. Sweating the night away oblivious. Stained dark clothes. I wonder whatever happened to? She gave me the sweetest kiss out of the blue. No never expected that. She was the one they all fancied and here was me getting the kiss. Heheheh but we were just good friends. Never felt any other caress or heat. She was so much there at the time. So. Hm. God those awful toilets. Stink. Stench. Cold. Outside down the alley way. Walking there excited. Filled with talk. Never ending chatter. Chatter chatter. Expectation? Disappointed? No not really. Holding hands. Dancing and talking. Always the dark backs of heads silhouetted against the light from the stage. Kind of like magic. Magic shamen. Rituals. Ritualising I suppose. Was it? Sometimes over a hundred in there. Jam packed. Couldn't move much. Used to find a seat on the backs of the benches at the back. Get out me Marlboro and enjoy the smoke. Adding to the smells of the crowd and the adrenaline. Real live music. And then. Yes. Parties. Endless stream. Walking walking. Talking. A guy taking photos. Yeah him. Used to watch him. Only a slight buzz from the drink. Not enough money for drinks. No need. No. Need.

"State Control. State Control. This is State Control…Beaten up behind closed doors…cuts and bruised ribs. Bloody mouth"

The state. State control. Seen it a few times. Bloody revolutions.
I don't want your revolution I want anarchy and peace. Heh.
Stuck on a loop in my head here now. State violence. Bloody
revolutions. That punk girl in London that time. Drunk almost
passed out. Lying across the path. She must have been cold. Her
face cold against the cold pavement. Almost oblivious. Then
those two coppers started giving her the hassle. Poking and
prodding. Asking. Asking her to move. And she gives it a fuck off
to them in her heavy French accent. Or was it Dutch? No
matter. Two coppers all big shiny footwear big hard men
shouting at a little girl really. She couldn't have been more than
seventeen. Like a small raggedy doll. All dressed in black
patchwork. Heh. Someone's little girl somewhere. And he has
his SPG mate with him. Trying to look hard? But is it state
controlled or people controlled? What makes a German citizen
push a Jew into a gas chamber? Is it state control? Sometimes
the kids aren't alright. Those coppers were so up for a fight.
Best way to start it by picking on a little girl. I watched as she
tried to explain she wasn't English and didn't understand. I
watched as the SPG thugs in a van slowly crawled closer
waiting for a fight. So hoping. Could see it in their eyes. Leers
on their faces. Holding their shields and batons at the ready.
Staring at the dirty punks outside their music venue squat. An
old ambulance station. Always filled with black, black, red,
green, spiky hair, dreadlocks, patchwork clothes, vegan hockey
boots, long black matted hair, some blonde spikes, huge. Heh.
Loved that scene. Dirty punks. No hippies. Just dirty punks.
Crass. Discharge. Antisect. Rudimentary Peni. Grind. Anarchy

peace and freedom. Real community feeling. Mostly so friendly. Crass logos everywhere. Flux stencils. Backs of leather jackets. Plastered with band names and logos. SO imaginative. Inventive. Grinding pumping sounds of Antisect drifting out to us as we negotiated with the coppers to let her go. Starting to build and brew now. People getting angry. Coppers winding us up. SPG van getting closer. Scary. Heh. I scared. Went back inside to see if I could find someone eloquent enough to deal with the coppers. Went back outside and she was gone. So exciting times. Down to London on the train. Squats. Flux and Steve Ignorant. All mixing with us. No gods. No masters. All in it together. No rock stars. Well. Not many. So friendly. Good times. Some bad times. Bad shit. Some dodgy squats. No water. No toilets. People acting and living in filth. Crazy. Some punks jumping on the bandwagon to get free food free lodgings and giving nothing back. Some great people. Vegan casseroles. Warming in a night so dark and cold. Talk of revolution. Anarchy. Peace. And freedom. Animal rights, human rights. Heh. All talking. Some action. Direct. Subversive. Dark in black clothes patchwork.

3:46 read the green fluorescent lights on the video recorder. He stands uneasily and wandered out into the kitchen and opens the fridge

Food? Empty.

Still alone now. Two days and two nights. No one to talk to. Just me here inside my own head. Sharing this space with him? With me. Many selves in here? Can pretend all different?

Looking around just alone. The walls, the ceiling, the shadows crossing the room as the light meanders in slowly, impossibly slowly. Making patterns and shapes.

He stares at the sink and the washing up.

That will be done one day. When I'm not here any more or in this mind. The cooker with pots and pans sitting waiting to be emptied. Cold greasy water.

He opens the lid of one pot and looks inside.

Thin grey gruel. Somehow that had passed for a meal some time in the past. So long ago. How many days?

He sighs and replaces the lid carefully.

Time flies, and my time crawls, like an insect, up and down the walls.

Anger. Somehow diffused.

He draws back the blind

The enclosed world of the garden. To go out onto the street was the thing, to live amongst the living again. To rub shoulders with the social of society. To do instead of just thinking. To live and be real.

He returns to the lounge and watches a couple walking silently home.

It was starting to get light already

Sun is trying to rise over the red-bricked buildings. Blood red sun.

The streets don't look so bad now.

The couple stop and kiss, he sneers cynically. Turns and flicks the hair from his face . It is lank and greasy .

Someone said I was pretty once. Who was it and when . I don't know. Got to leave the house soon to get some more fags . The shops open in a couple of hours. Then out before the people are up, alone as usual.

He slumps down into the armchair.

I almost feel sorry for myself. Stagnating living hand to mouth.

He wears odd socks, a grey sweatshirt ripped and black jeans shiny with filth . He rubs the arms of the chair.

Soothing myself . To sleep just one night without the tingling and the pressure of that tightly coiled snake , black and slimy , curled in my brain slowly expanding and shifting as it devours my vitality ever. A click . A flame . Another cigarette . Burning down slowly as I sit and watch.

He takes few drags but sucks hard. Chasing the smoke in.

Nicotine making my head light and knees weak.

His eyes shudder.

My mind spins dizzy. Am I dead?

The ash falls into the ashtray. And the dog end is tossed casually into the bin. The room is bright now, another beauty of a day, cool now but heat-ridden later.

5:12

He sighs.

He is thinking back, remembering again. He is looking up at the ceiling. Looking for cobwebs.

Thinking of spiders.

He rubs his eyes a little.

Any alcohol here? Doubt it. Before this time. When we were young.

He laughed to himself a little.

I can recall it all. Like a dream come true. Not only are they from a grim and dark northern town. All working class lads. A genuine cult band. Possibly Nazis [this could possibly produce an endless source of debate and discussion, not to mention lots of possible research], were relatively obscure, had lyrics which could be read in so many wonderfully adolescent ways but also the lead singer was dead.

Not only is he dead but it was death by suicide.

And then, here it comes; it wasn't just a casual rock and roll suicide. This guy had hanged himself on the eve of his bands tour which would have broken the states.

And what would they have done then . Where would they be in twenty years . Like the rolling stones . I knew that .

*Had been there and back . Travelled as I was through all time
and space . So love me what would they have done . Where
would they have gone had he not died . Would he have become
an old rocker living off his youth . Now his youth was framed in
the perfection of photography . Those wonderful black and white
images . Snowy scenes of Macclesfield .*

But there was still more.

*He had hanged himself. This wasn't soft. Not some passive slip
into oblivion from booze, drugs, tablets or even a slit wrist lying
in a warm bath drinking whiskey and smoking a joint.*

He. Hanged. Himself.

*Like a final dramatic violent statement of intent. This. Is. Not.
Working. Which ever way you look at this its one of the hardest
ways out. This is taking death whole and staring it in the face
and breathing it in. Dark, dank, seductive odour. Tying your
rope, tie, flex, whatever. Putting it around your own neck,
whichever way you do it. Touching the thing, holding the thing
which is about to end your ability to reason, see, breathe.
Holding that self-murder weapon. Adjusting it! Getting into
position. Almost a complete ceremonial act. Could you really do
this drunk? No.*

No.

So taking it full on. No hiding from it. This is going to be an end. And possibly it hurts like hell. So if you fall using your weight, kicking away the stool you are standing on. Does that hurt? Is it a fair way out?

He lights another cigarette, inhales and looks out of the window into the pale morning light for a few moments. Then he strides over and picks out an album and studies the cover. White background with a black and white photograph on of a mausoleum.

So many years ago I found you. So much pleasure from music you brought me.

Music more than art.

And what really would I prefer to lose? Eyes or Ears. Well not either but the sense?

Inhaling long and hard. Exhaling the same. Breathing in the hot smoke now, lung-filling brain sustaining. Fidgeting and unable to sit still now. Insects crawling my flesh. Scratching at them. Staring at patterns in the carpet. Staring at the ash building up. The cigarette glow swelling during the inhale as the paper and tobacco burn more brightly. Addict. Addicted.

Addiction. Addicted. So desperate for that cannabis hit. Looking and waiting. Selling clothes. Selling books. Selling anything. You get desperate. Needy. Its not the diamorphine addiction. Different. Not the aching throbbing sickness. Just a need. A space to fill. To seek oblivion.

Walking, dealer to dealer. All day sometimes. Nothing doing. Until you find someone who is waiting for the deal to come off. For the money holder to come back. All smiles and happiness.

"Five minutes and your almost there."

Its like sitting in a room filled with ghosts. Shades of real people. Some waiting for hash, others speed, acid, whatever. All fidgeting. Ever moving. Shifting from on e point to another mentally and physically in the same place. Nervous glances exchanged. Small nervous smiles exchanged. Mindless chit-chat. Expectation rises each time we hear footsteps approaching and the collective slump when the footsteps continue. Not stopping.

This is a dealer's house. Most things you would find in a normal house are gone. There's no TV, no radio, no stereo, very little furniture.

Frankly I'm surprised there is still a bed in here.

Addicts sell everything.

Walked into the kitchen once to make a cup of tea. The room watched as I got up. Some confused. Newcomer breaking the rules. The trail of expectation. One of them opened a can of Special Brew. The *snap* of the ring pull a bullet shot. Others looked at the can with envy. Not usual to share. No addicts share.

In the kitchen, no kettle, opening cupboards empty one by one. In one the remains of the full set of crockery been given to the dealer so many years ago. Before the parents had died of old age and disappointment. All left now was a single stained cup, the saucer long since broken and a bowl. Sitting in juxtaposition weirdly a bag of sugar, unopened, and a full table salt. A couple of tea bags lay next to the cup. Other cupboards making me smile. Rotted vegetables and broken half useless cooking utensils randomly spread about. Eventually there was that small saucepan.

Turns smiling to the sink. Old takeaway carton.

Not from a real addict. Real addicts don't waste money on food. Its just not done. All your money is tied up with your addiction. Nothing wasted on the luxuries of normal daily life. All is consumed by addiction. It burns you up. Fills each and every day from waking to sleeping. That moment if your lucky enough when oblivion happens. Day's work is done. Filling body and soul with the drugs, drink, sex, pornography or whatever.

Your needs.

A couple of chipped mugs. Not much else. Piled up. All in the sink. Plenty of beer cans though. Cigarette butts. ANyhything counts as an ash-tray here. A brand new album cover been used to roll up on. Left by a casual visitor looking to score weed for the weekend. A stranger in a strange lnad. Weekend drugs. Entertainment value only. Suspect. Watched.

Or is he a pig?

Turn the tap on. It coughs and spits out water. Put it on the stove. Cooker top caked with grease and slime. Hasn't been cleaned in months, if ever. Addicts don't waste their energy on housework. Not house proud. Too much like hard work. Interferes. Minimal existence. You choose your drug and escape if you can. That's the goal.

"Day in day out, day in day out."

Carpets crusted with mess and spilt drinks, burn marks. Holes. Caked with grime. Walls smeared with hand marks. Dirt. Finger marks. Old signs of tea spilled down. Beer, Coffee.
Never break the cycle. Day on day. Monday. Every day becomes every day. No turkey for Christmas. Addiction fills you up. All energy used to satisfy that need to sink into unthinking oblivion. Escape. Escapology. Addiction is escaping the bullshit.

"Its all bullshit."

*Like running from the earth to the sun at full tilt. Or driving your
car into a motorway bridge. Its your only focus. Only reason to
live.*

*Water boils and I pour it over the teabags in the broken mug and
make a thin weak black tea. Sip it. Walk back into the waiting
room. Glance across grey unseeing faces, unkempt hair, half
grown beards, matted hair, Oddments of clothing, Unmatched
unwashed clothes. Cheap clothes. Charity shop clothes. Bed, no
sheets on it just an old tatty sleeping bag. A gas fire half hanging
off the wall. Holes in the wall. Curtains grey with filth. Windows
so dirty you cant see out. Paintwork peeling. Dog hairs stuck to
the carpet from a dog dead years ago.*

*The small expectant crowd looks up. Three old wino girls
waiting on some smack have managed to get Special Brew to
share his can. Not just the one in his hand but one hidden away
inside his huge black overcoat. Designed for shoplifting. Like
three witches surrounding him. Caressing him. Special Brew
must be new to this enjoying the attention. Others watching this
scene replaying too. Glaring. Waiting. Looking always for the
bagman. The money holder. To get back and spread out the joy.
Heh. Big job being the bagman on a run like this. Must have
three hundred quid on him. Nasty. One time bagman didn't get
back and he was thrown into the sewers half conscious . Nasty.*

Heh. Carrying all that money. Making the score and getting the gear. Then that long walk back. Never doing that again. Terrified. So scared. So scared and cold and lonely. Watching every person a suspect going to take my score. Coming back from King's heath. In the winter that time. Cold wet. Rain. Skin soaking. Shivering. Scared every car that drives past is the pigs. Or worse. Other addicts.

Shot by both sides. Back to Nature. I can't go on like this.

Pigs want to know where you got it from. Punters want to know how much money and what you holding. If your lucky they let you live. Kill you for thirty quid easy. No safety net. No insurance. Carrying a gun that time. No idea how to use it. Just. So. Scared.

And then the door opens and the bagman walks in and shakes his head. Some hash but nothing more. Money is passed around and back. Small packs of hash are handed over like rations. Within five minutes the room is empty again and we are left in silence just him and me. Talk through a few old memories of times before we were trapped. Times when we had freedom. School days. Girlfriends. Gigs. Music. Cars. Money. Life before the addiction. Then he makes a huge bong mix, lights inhales and slips into oblivion on the bed. I let myself out quietly.

That's addiction. Not so long ago.

Snap. Back to the present.

Whatever that means.

Back to here and me now and you vicarious observer. Looking at me? You looking at me? Black on white, sepia. White on black. So many centuries hanging between us now. Five hundred years at least. Swimming through that cold black void maybe even?

The grey man at the wheel looks around . Searching for some skirt . Crawling the kerb he's got the money all he needs is a body . He hates kissing them . Uses them . A commodity to be bought and sold like so much meat at a cattle market .

Butcher his flies hang open . A big fat frog in a big fat car . He cares for no one except himself . Racist . Sexist . Bigot . He smirks as he catches sight of an old wino girl Katy staggering and tottering up the Kettering Road. Her leather jacket open her eyes glossy yet dull . A bottle clutched half empty . He drives smoothly over . Asks if she wants a lift . She nods and steps in . Blind plush velour interior . Even leather . He puts some music on as they drive and offers her more drink . Vodka .

Aahh she glugs down the clear liquid and they are gone .

Cause and effect. Ripples from a stone splashing spreading across the cool mirror surface of a big pond. Increasing regular sine wave decreasing in power. Yet never becoming. Nothing. The power is transferred. It's just the form which changes. Energy cannot be created or destroyed. It exists in perpetuity. Always. No end. No change. We will one day be two atoms, you and I chasing each other across the black of the universe, cheating entropy. Waiting. Love so strong that we cheat the fear and the blackness of the void. Stars made from the souls of the dead powering the universe. Existence and knowing, comprehension much more important to the entropy creeping towards us so slowly that we cant see it coming. Entropy not powered by love. Love overcoming. Love is all.

So hard purging myself like this every day. Stories all I have left now. Memories like small cameos in my head. Like the scenes from a big film that will make me rich one day. Living life in the third person at times. Seeing it from afar. Obvious why?

And I'm in love with you. Obsessed with obsession. I opened up my eyes. I kissed her face I kissed her hair. It tasted sweet with perfume. But shes gone. They are all gone. What really makes a kiss so special? The tingling feeling of electricity passing between two stars, giant epic colossal colonies. Burning stars circling each other as small as two atoms and as large as you can ever possibly imagine.

Inhale.

Those two stars circling held in each other's gravity unable to escape. Not able to feel any more just empathic. Capable of just empathy as their huge mass keeps them spinning. Born at the beginning of time? No. Created at death? Everlasting love conquers it all. Yeah. Cheats death. Cheats entropy. Love is the law. Stronger than death of course. Must be.

Exhale.

Leave that hollow carcass behind wont we? Surely? Then to be free to chase across the stars immortal. Stand on the top of the greatest mountains in the solar system and see the ice cool seas of sulphur. Stand whip lashed in the never ending hurricanes and gigantic storms on Jupiter, Fly way out past the final planet and...

Inhale.

Beat. Beat. Thump.

Its still in there pumping away. Keeping me alive.

I need an answer . No imagination cluttering up this world . Visual images of the past haunting me. Everyday filled with ghosts pain guilt and suffering . A heart of crystal steel . No answers are coming your way .

You need faith . Leap into that void . Cross across . I am not going to make it that easy . And you don't deserve it . I sneer . You are pathetic. Selfish. God made and god seeking .

I was conceived and born in the church of holy christ jesus where he was christened . The lifting music the flowing purple robes the colours the vibrancy shimmering with gold and white holy steel flesh . The heavy scent of frankincense and myrrhish smouldering candleflames flickering across the dusty white walls . Icons of weeping saints and tear-choked Marys crying in everlasting joy .

Rowonrow of chairs nailed together to form pews like in the proddy churches . But more refined and decent . Somehow English Catholicism . Weeping instead of a strong brew and a kind word . Jesus nailed to his cross . Fantastic story of martyrdom love hate jealousy . Crying tears for us sinners and sinned upon . He store down upon the young, at him first then me . Just asking . A simple beauty in the clear eye . I was young and foolish . I tried shouting . but it didn't work . I looked at Jesus a grim tear in his eye the blood from his crown trickling across that noble cheek .

His thin taut body hanging limp .

What was Jesus thinking then?

At that final moment? He looked bitter to me . Frightened and confused . Tortured and abused a mockery of a saviour . Too human . Real . Alive and living . For one instant he looked most of all to be angry . He questioned and twisted . Gasping in his personal sacrifice . Gods son on earth . Come   to raise us up . He must have looked down at us insects gathered around his feet and wept and laughed . He must have thought was it all worthwhile .

That was our first lesson together.

In bed aged seven I lay on the rack . Fever sweeping through me. A rushing hurricane of dreams heats and visions . And incredible pain scorching my smooth belly . The hallucinations terrified me. Spiders crawling my flesh. Wasps buzzing mercilessly. Trapped in my hair. Saints lecturing me and ghosts and sinners imploring Fools laughing Terrors ships ghosts witches goblins. Endless every day and night for over a month . My cosmos was at an end . The lines of fate were twisted and tangled a skein of wool looped around a spinning dancer beautiful . Prancing ballerina lost in time to age and death . Mother sat up with me glorious shimmering holy lily of my valley sleeping fitfully in a bedside chair . Worried sick herself crying and waiting . The most beautiful lady in the world . Not skin and flesh but the golden angelity of the divine , mother is so perfect humanity . Love.

And now it's the summer of nineteen eighty two. I was a poet then, once, filled with hopes and emotions. In that strange summer. Can still remember that first kiss.

He sits up and sips at his cup of cold black tea and looks around. He stands and paces to the desk. His writing desk. He stares idly into the twilit hall as he passes. A casual glance. He searches for something on the desk. Finds it and lifts it.

My precious book of poems.

He flicks from page to page.

Searching feverish haste.

He tuts.

He turns and reads aloud

"Revelations,   a mirror by a stream,   a sleeping Lancelot, a knight in a dream. The lady of lights lips caress his brow, his eyes are opened he sees her glow. The knight emerges, scarred, but not man yet, a boy no longer , yet he knows not what . He lies no more to look at the sky, knows no more of simple joy. The mirror shears the stream. The voice of Yahweh enters the dream. The warriors lay down their swords, as the mirror shatters into shards. Of glass to pierce a thousand hearts."

That summer was a dream . She appeared like a faint hope a chance to quench the fire burning and devouring my spirit . One kiss that was all that was needed to change things . A warm summer eve after an eye-opening night drinking and laughing . Two pints later full of confidence we talked . She was older than me by four years . An age of eternal otherness . She wanted my love . The kisses and his tender touch of lover so young first love lover rare . Tender touch soft embrace .

These shabby words reveal so little . And make me so cross . She there in the half light standing by the names of the forgotten dead . Heroes of a different war the time of grand death . Honourable war . We kissed . My first . Something to never forget . An old man remembers caresses fleshy waists and soft chests and thighs . We run away . When we think of her we cry . Saddened our child lost only metaphysical . Unreal child of someone elses seed . Not his or mine . A brief moment over so quickly yet stained forever now . In the present . things moved in a whirl a vortex of time and living .

I lie trapped in this cell celibate monk . Events places chance encounters a series of fleeting pictures framed against a backcloth of devoted narcissicism.

There was no time to think . Only time to do .

Repercussions were never considered the idea was to do . What felt right . I think we've lost that now . Now we plot and we suffer trying to make it all right . But it hardly ever is . We refuse to cross the void of like and enter the depths of love . Everything is dark now heavy with feeling a type of premeditated emotion only loving when its right .

I taught you to run the race without looking to the finish . Its the race which counts .Not winning or losing sadness or regrets .We fear harming others and forget ourselves .

Life goes on ever down and up . Cycles of love and hate . Aborted love affairs ended wrong . Too early . Too late christened children will wake and stare at their mothers and love for all time . This don't change . Like we change .

Loving humanity tires .

One summer warming morning I sat captivated in adoration staring at father's favourite orange curtains backlit by the sun . Large golden flowers patterned the material . Head cocked to one side . Listening.

*My eyes danced back and forth over the fabrics smooth ululating
surfaces and planes drifting in a gentle breeze . "I love you
mum" And we hugged. "I love dad too... and Nathan" "Who is
Nathan?" mum had asked casually. "He's my brother of course
silly!" My special brother hidden away up here in my head.
Mum had looked so sad and turned away hiding the few soft and
salty tears which rolled down her face. She was thinking of how
all my brothers and sisters had died before ever really entering
this world. Carried away before taking a breath. Small tiny...
things... no... babies. Her babies taken away from her before
their time. Unborn.*

*I could listen to him for hours . Talking as equals . Discussing
the lives of the saints and the martyrs . He swore to me that he
could feel the strength of their power and love flooding through
his veins . He felt the awe of their will . Was protected and pure .
He was blessed .*

He spoke aloud addressing the room, "caressing the marble and
stone down there, in the grave, tied down , I wish you were here
to protect me in this lonely exile . You running away. Leaving
me to face this mess. This corrupt bastard life. Old England's
dead. Forget it. Kick the fucking corpse for all I care. I'm just
sick of it. And you"

He won't go away . He is so deep in me. I am so deep in him . Knows I hold his memories for him . Our memories . My mind coiled up inside his together forever . We two are strong . I am controller . He is controlled . But we do . Do we . Who is here inside this space of thoughts . What spliced us together . Talking talking . Thinking thinking . Together not together apart and yet one joined .

He lays back silent for some time and then his eyes open slowly a tiresome look on his face, a sad look. He stares at the walls now.

Same as ever.

He looks at the faces of the two paintings of Jesus and Mary which both had tears in their eyes.

Seems right. Beautiful lovingly hand-painted onto glass, works of a dying craft. The only thing I own that I really love.

Now. Passed down to me from the past, great grandmother long since deceased and consumed by our planet. Body now so much less than human, in pieces, devoured and one with the beautiful spinning blue and white globe hung in the blackness.

A crown of thorns suffering shame with dignity and honour.
(dulce et decorum est) Thats the answer . Learning how to carry
on through the pain and the blood such a perfect sorrow .
Maybe the odd regret that more time was not available . But we
all run from time and hide from it . It seeks us out all kills us off
one by one . We rush about filling time marking the card and
passing on filling spaces in time the gaping hole of existence .
Never thinking making noises like the hollow shallow men of
history trying so hard not to be alone .

Alone.

A stab in my chest, asurging , arising rush of panic and
paranoia , tears in my eyes. Swelling as I sat thinking of the
future . Pained at the realisation that those pictures I so love
would be smashed and shattered in an outburst of anger and
regret, and rejection. Even more frightening realizing its my
fault. Powerless to stop it. Pictures of never ever ending dreams
locked up and spat out, heading rapidly to that point in time , a
nexus a zenith a nadir a time a moment of then. The shouting
and screaming accusations regrets pain anger anxiety loveless
feelings based on the faith of the past and the experience of the
present.

On edge now, walking the razor's edge, slipping into sorrow.

Lights dancing on the ceiling, reflecting shapes and figures that once could have been prancing horses. Now things so obscene that I shut my eyes to make them go away. But they won't. A rushing sound fills the room with white-noise regularity a falling into sound, getting louder phasing right and left up and down.

He tries to stand but cannot , and collapses , blackened out , unconscious sweating , he looks fit to vomit , green skin lank lifeless hair sticks to unkempt unwashed body reverence in its isolation . Clothes dirty. He lifts his head from the bluegreen carpet arid smiles weakly and almost sweetly. His head drops, thoughts flood in without check and confuse and confound.

God I need a smoke.

This world tries to drag me down with overbearing gravity, the metaphysics and politicacy of reality a burden borne with deep pain. Weak chest muscles, the heart pumping fast, quickquick now, stalling and continuous in decay, and each beat means one less.

He gets, up and lifts a packet of biscuits, slowly removes one, places it carefully in his mouth and chews silently and gently.

Crumbs drop from the corners of his mouth and fall, spiralling down toward earth, as they do catching the light, still frames on a roll of film, twisting tiny golden snowflakes cascading suspended hanging briefly in the ether. Somehow they begin to look more real important beautiful stunning than idle concepts of love and death.

He seems to fight the nausea. Pushes back the emptiness and the bile in his stomach. Stands and pads over to the TV and switches it on, noiseless as usual the green furry against the blue and red. Images flicker across the screen, as channels are studied and dismissed rapidly onebyone .He turns but leaves it on - news breakfast TV.

He moves across and turns the Hi-Fi on again and puts a cassette into the lower , slightly older deck , turns on the various components and watches , still fascinated as the different light blink on , the music begins .

An unguarded moment . Every song brings back a memory and inspires an emotion, some to be cherished , some instantly dismissed , those that pass away are never forgotten , just stored for use later. The sound of music the greatest trigger of memory emotion. Taste and smell also the triggers of times past. Times long long ago.

There is an old biscuit. He spies it. Studies it's texture. Stares at it. Looks at it as if he is looking at a tiny universe held between his fingers picking it up. A few mouthfuls of stale biscuit later the nausea has passed.

I touched your golden hair it tasted of sweet perfume . The room was empty as I stepped in from the cold gravel of grave . Your golden lips raised up to me will one day be nothing more than words in a book . A fading memory of sweetness and light with warm tender heart . Taken out and used in sad quiet moments of recollection . Nostalgia .

Chelsea girl had a heavier introduction . Guitar growl groping for compassion and heroin. Time to go. Time to crawl blinking into the sun. Costumes would be donned like gowns and knightly armour. Armed and ready prepared for battle. Antisect so heavy it hurts . An endless seamless wall of perfection noise wise. So love that. Never heard anything better. Live one long song, flowing and ebbing from one to the next. One long set. No stopping between songs. Seen them practice like that. Working on the cross over points. Pol smacking out those drum sounds. Wink and his funky bass. Quiet Wink. Rich and Pete. Intimidating. Aggressive. Overwhelming. Shouting and singing. And Lippys guitar a sonic wall of noise. Like a slab of sound. Making a new way.

My dragons would eat up St George's in a trice .

Are we all Eliot's stuffed hollow men . Scared crows . Sacred cows . Shit for brains with our dicks in our hands . Castration complexes filling me in. Tying me down while trying to lift me up . Two buckets in a well .

A hand-me-down-dress bought for you with the last of my dole money. Albums U2. Magazine. Joy Division. Crass. Flux. Discharge, Husker Du. So much glory in eight miles high. Takes you so high. Takes you to the limit and back. Such animal emotion growling angry singing. NO. Not singing. Wailing. Like the most despair ever. First time I heard that it really did send a shiver down me spine. Still does. The sound of beauty and despair twiseted together on the same loom. And what did you do. Laughed and said what will I do with these old rags when Monday comes around. **Too many references**. *Too much poetry ingrained in our heads. Unable to make a clear new thought? So much pressed into us? Maybe you sneered at my most precious gift. Or maybe I imagined it.*

The silence at the end of the song drags him back to harsh reality, he forgets the past again, and remembers the weaknesses of today.

There will be a revolution. Now. But this will not be televised. This will be a private revolution. The most powerful kind of epiphany is coming and I am waiting for it. Just biding my time now.

Need to put some shoes on. Looks nice. A really nice morning. Couple of quid get some fags.

See someone. God see anyone now. Strawberry china girl in fields of azure bathing in a field of poppies. Melancholia of music certain strains and patterns. Like books and words. And thoughts. A language beyond me. A balloon floating. Find me sanctuary and lock me in monklike. Someone please do this.

He is clearly thinking back again. Always lost in his memories.

Time alone I cant help but swim around in the stream of times past and present more than the future I now know will come to pass. Thoughts as a stream of true conciousness are all that we are. We don't have heroic meaning in our lives and myself as the hero somehow in a story is ridiculous. Heh.

He smiles a wry smile. Pacing the room. Pacing. Upstairs now. His hand is holding the hand rail and feeling every single tiny bump or change in texture. That kind of self studied memory creation born out of doing the same thing over and over again. Like running your tongue across your teeth knowing exactly how each and every one of them feels and fits together. And the horror and shock when a tooth falls out or is extracted as your tongue feels inside the gap time and time again. Seeking that which has been lost.

Now in the bathroom he unzips his trousers and begins to piss into the toilet bowl. Looking around the bathroom as he does so. Staring at the bath taps, one of which is still dripping. Each droplet of water in itself a tiny universe created in a tiny big bang at the tap and living for an eternity as it falls through time and explodes into a million shattered atoms upon impact with the bath itself.

Wonder what it like live inside the water or under the sea? Staring up at the light. Swimming and living in the darkness. Heh. Yeah. Those big dark shapes again. Is that now or later? Dark shapes. Kind of that hidden thing. That scary thing? Where you scare yourself? Like horror movies or scary books. Dracula. That one. Cant recall. Dark gothic writings and ramblings.

He stares down at his piss arcing down into the bowl. Directing it around the bowl. Playing games with his stream of dark yellow, almost brown piss. Looking down at it he realised this was also a part of the disease. Diagnosed a few days before. Probably the result of an excessive lifestyle.

Excessive… that's one way to put it. Drink. Mainly drink. Really excessive drink battering my kidneys and liver. No alcohol for a month. No way. But only a pint now and again. Living so close to the pub makes it hard. Must hide this. Yellow eyes do give it away a bit. And yellowing skin And the piss.

Another timeless moment. Another starting point. Another set of memories to construct and put together into time and context.

Ahh. When the first wave of punk came along in the summer of 77. 11 going on 12. Listening to Radio One and Top of the Pops. Mainly the Sex Pistols, The Skids and The Stranglers, never any punk on daytime national radio. Too young to have known of John Peel. Anyhow 10 oclock way past my bedtime.

Loving that punk music the way here was something that was openly rebellious and was designed to piss of your parents. Not that I hated mine at all. This new music filled with real energy, angst and hit that chord in me. I could pretend more. But really just the raw power and the sound, especially of the pounding drums and buzz-saw guitars.. The vocals spat out and the sneering cynicism of Johnny Rotten. He just looked like he wanted to stick two-fingers up at the status quo. And that made sense. Not completely. But there was something. The clothes. The hairstyles. Freedom. Individuality.

Buying records? No way. No money

Then as punk's wave diminished I followed the general fashion and moved on to the New Romantic. Then a new group of friends and turned back onto punk. Sitting at Clifford Mill House till late into the night. Crass. Flux. The Damned. Magazine. Understanding and reading the ideology of Crass and Anarchy.

All this happens in an instant. Memories flowing across the mind's eye in an instant. Not taking time. Images and pictures. Scenes replaying. Scene after scene. Moment after moment rolling all into one reel of film. Seamless.

The piss still flowing out into the bowl.

Must clean this out before she gets home. Really must. And the bath. Can I? Think I have time? What. No rush. Hm

Mum the devout Catholic believing that God was in everything. Must give her a call. Or pop up and see her. She. So much made me. Made my world. Times we fell out. Stabbing me deep pangs. When she will be gone. God in the wind and the rain. All men and women equal. No class or colour believing in freedom and peace and that really Jesus was a Communist.

That summer of 1982 in Scotland to visit family friends. Angus and Johnny. Heavy metal. Saving my money until we found a record shop in Edinburgh. Buying Punk and Disorderly and Never Mind the Bollocks. Playing them incessantly.

Returning to Northampton joining the sixth form and then leaving. Glorius new beginning. New dawn. Bright and golden times.

Piss finished he flushes the toilet. Stares around. Looks in the mirror.

Definitely skin too yellow. Eyes too yellow. Not right. That worn now twisting itself around. What is it? Something in my brain. Growing and feeding on me. A particle started and moved into the brain tumouring. Reprogrammed and now growing a lump inside my head. Jaundice.

Tired he turns and moves slowly towards his bedroom, goes in and looks round again. As if he is recording this for some purpose later on in life. Not like he is now living.

Why am I recording these moments? Not living now? In limbo. A character in a story? I am not living. Its all silence as he drifts in and out of overwhelming memories. Crashing over me like tidal waves sucking me under and away from the now and to the past. The then. Observed by the other. Observing the other. Both of them.

Both of us.

He moves further into the room and gently folds the sheets on the bed making it neat.

Funny how suicides like to tidy up before committing their final act.

He smiles again and feels inside his pocket.

Cigarettes and a lighter.

He takes out a cigarette and lights it moving towards the window to look out over the back garden.

Really the front garden.

The stranger is still out there. Standing and watching.

Occasionally he takes out a notebook and scribbles something down. A stranger dressed from head to foot in black. A large hat obscuring his face. He smokes as well. The small pile of dog-ends is building up by his feet. He has been there for two days on and off.

Wonder what he doing there. Staring up at me as I look down at him. Quite brazen. No fear. Wonder.

They stare at each other a moment of shared silence.

An energy passing between us. Is this going to be a war between us? The electricity. The moment of contact. Both smoking and mirroring each other's moves. Possibly a shadow?

War does not pay.

Being young and being free.

No responsibilities.

Great weather. Social explosion going to see bands and talking to like minded people. Although painfully shy. I mostly kept myself to myself at those gigs. Just wanting to hear the music so loved. Felt like freedom. Felt exciting and vibrant. Anyone could form a band and lots of people did. No matter if you can play or not. Just need the imagination and confidence to get up and do it.

It felt like we could change the World. Crass were massive. As were Discharge. And Antisect and Flux. Crass were still singing their angry hymns. And so were many more. Still the black and white records came and we read their covers and looked at the pictures and read the slogans and we could see through the lies spread around us by the men in suits. We listened. Read. And understood. Sometimes.

We were fighting the great evil of Margaret Thatcher and Nuclear War. Felt good to be part of the tribe that was standing up against oppression and actually saying something in the music and the words.

Such a romantic view of the past. Looking back at a brighter time. And still only 24. Or 23? No idea now. Lost still in this time stream I cannot escape from. Mostly just being young and filled with energy made it exciting at the time. But was it?

He backs away from the window and walks down the stairs again. This time the left hand following and studying via touch as a sense the reverse signs and signals sent out by its woodyness into his fingertips and his palm. Like a negative photo of the memory created on the way up. Such was his intelligence that all these things flowed into him as a matter of course. But then this is the same for all of us. Just that most of us don't notice or comprehend that it is happening. We walk about with so much constant noise and chatter.

> *She is such a pretty girl,*
> *Her shape fits well into a mould.*
> *Her mind removed, her body's sold,*
> *She does exactly what she's told.*
> *And he is such a brave young man,*
> *If his brain can't then violence can.*
> *His mind was drained since life began*
> *Of the compassion he once had.*

The words echoing around inside his head just seemed to fit him. Then do we fit things to ourselves or is it a co-incidence? We struggle to look for things that fit into our flow of life and time.

He walks back into the living room.

His eyes wandered the room, searching for his elusive shoes.

Not there.

He moves into the hall and opens one of the cupboard doors, casting the narrow corridor into deep shadow of partial darkness. They were on top of his coats.

How pathetic. All piled up in disarray a lifetime of second hand items and gifts not one thing I had gone out and bought because it was really wanted. A fugitive black coat from grandfather. Old and worn but with a certain level of style.

He brushes the coat down and gingerly puts it on and squats down to do up his boot laces, looking pleased he turns to face the full length mirror facing the kitchen door.

Maybe shave. Maybe not. Money lighter keys.

A figure looms in the garden, he freezes and stands stock still not one breath is taken, panic mounts and rises, the shape moves closer to the front door, there is   a rattle   at the letterbox as two letters slip through and fall onto the shiny tiles by the doormat.

Clean those again today.

Step inside this is the   way step inside.

Two brown envelopes, one white lie motionless.

Here's a challenge. What will they tell me? Worth opening or looking at them?

When am I?

He bends down as if to pick them up, stopping just before feeling the texture of the paper of the envelopes on his fingertips.

Paper like dryness and sterility a potential fire trap to be avoided.

He picks up the white one.

The other two are bills, nothing to concern me now. Such a precious gift in my hand.

He examines it more closely and sees the tear stains that have smudged the handwritten address on the front, the ink has formed pools in the contours of the flesh of the paper.

Has it really been here for two long days already? No can't have been. Must have been the rain. Here she comes again.

I want to open it and feel some love for a change.

He drops the letter and lets it slip and spin to the floor.

Selfish. That greatest need. Filling and eating at me. That nicotine flood in my lungs, the lightness in my head. That intake which makes a sense of everything. And then I can start to think again. Breathe and eat like I should have been doing for the last three months.

Interregnum of holy clouded joyless asphyxia. Machine guns.

He stares through the frosted glass of the front door, at the light, the brightness and sits down on the bottom step head in hands staring at his boots, bestrapped and falling apart.

Thirty bloody quid.

Look again at the light outside, without the darkness of this heart, like Marlowe looking ever forward whilst the rest of the world looks back, like characters in a play. Self sacrificial lambs. The world's brightness, spinning and floating through space this little blue ball, humming and whirring, full of glorious life, insects scurrying hereandthere, making ends meet.

O glorious sun golden sun spinning in the heavens floating in the ether. Maybe they've got it wrong. Walking on the suns surface. Now that's a thing. All it takes is to open the door and walk out. Four days. A long time alone. Ghosts and daemons. Memories like the corner of my mind hidden away safeless and useless. Now.

Like something I rehearsed in my dreams.

A drunken stupor with two virgins. I acting the sage though just as scared as you. Frightened together. We wanted a union there on the dark cold floor. I don't know what it could mean our two bodies awkward and angular my clumsy hands seeking. Filled with the zeal and zest of an autodidact. Caressing me with hidden feelers and textures your back smooth. Like we rehearsed in a dream. Many dreams. Some lost others rediscovered some yet to happen. I just wished. Falling stars blurred at the edges with feminine curves in the half-darkness. Your smooth skin was dark and brown almost orange in the light falling from the outside streetlamp. Your belly lit up and the darkness and softness lower. Could almost see the bones holding you together.

I failed with you. My body shudder and screams no.

My mind is quiet now keeping its peace.

That was as close as I got then. Sharing a cigarette after. Not romance. Economy. Both of us trying to laugh it off. She became sick slumped in the big old armchair by the table lamp in the alcove . I tried to watch the telly. She repeating over and over the words I will never hear again in this life. She sobbed and pleaded later until they   came and took her home I was scared.

I was so young, or so it seemed to me.

He muttered as he stretched his hand out toward the door handle.

Dizzy hazy cold hot and miserable in this self imposed exile.
Cold. Clammy against the heat of the previous two weeks. A
death in June or July is rare except from the fires of forest.
There is a breeze too. Can smell and taste it on my tongue. At
the back of my throat, even through the door.

He turns the handle and pulls the door open, wincing at the daylight, taking out the tortoiseshell sunglasses from his pocket and putting them on.

Papers danced in the spirited air, shuffling whirled back and forth, his eyes followed their slow movements, circling in minor cyclones their chanting filled him. Reality and fancy were becoming increasingly meshed, taking only a slight action to avert his thought, change the rationale and the direction. Feelings and pain would surface again.

in in th dp

in th dp mid winter

in th dp mid

in th firm nird ham

i feel lk brthing and birthng unguard

He steps across the threshold into early morning sunlight , the concrete garden messy as usual , one of the plant pots casually rolling in the breathy wind making small arcs on the slabs , its contents spilled , earth and soil . A small sapling in his path rocking gently windshaken.

The big ginger cat Genghis stalked the wall, stopping to stare affronted at this shallow carcass, it sat and looked up, toward the rising sun, the fur on its face being rustled and blown.

I'll be sad to see you go. Sad end for a nice cat. Enjoy the day while you can. God bless you Genghis. Who thought up that name. You march proud up there don't let them keep you in .Die like a warrior, you don't want to be found in this greygrey town.

The cat slumped down then sprang without grace onto the porch and seemed to smile, a sad knowing look a smile   of expression, guru. Swami he began to lick   between his toes stretching them out on his back now searching for dirt.

He turns and pushes the door shut and pulls it to double check it is locked.

Its really just a question of honesty .

The invisible airwaves are crackling with light , smell the new summer coming with an hint of autumn as it approached its dying end .

The whole world would sigh on a morning like that . Its a question of freewill after all . I will always choose it over your petty timid ideologies and patterns of social change . There is no one with the right to tell you what to do . No law means anything.

Genghis is gone two years past . Times inconsistency . Those events in trying to be recalled together suffer under the repetition of tongues .

One day I shall be purged and tell you what I've seen

*Bullets start chasing **me.***

He paces evenly across the garden and steps past the rotting gate into the concrete stairlanding turns right and continues down and round finally ending in the side street , looking at the old shed in the middle of the car park , all of which would be demolished to make way for a fancy car showroom in a few months time .

Sitting in a room with demons. Just seventeen years old but a few ago now looking down at the brass mirror trailed with the pinky white traces of amphetamine sulphate. Whizz. Two crusty snails trails for me.

Never have a bad trip on speed.

Smiling happy. Taking a crisp pound note out of me jacket pocket the texture of the paper in hand obsessive joy. Not soiled old notes used screwed up in the hands of bus conductors. My notes have to be new. The feel of the paperlinen fresh and crisp and new. Yes. Like that. Foldable and untouched.

He carried on walking leftright whilst he considered the events of then. That time. Time spent looking into hell. Sunshine warm on his face. Cars passing in slow motion again. Light-headed and sometimes dizzy. White soft clouds scudding across the sky slowly. The pavement hard, so hard under his feet. So real.

Gently rolling that paper into a thin tube and bending down to inhale the powders onto the membranes. Pulling the rough powders up. Wow. Just wow and nothing less than that.

Speed cascading across my membranes infusing me with stolen adrenaline borrowed from chemical properties. A new type of raw power and energy texture sharp like glass or ice steel. Sanding the soft flesh. Burning houses down. The pain and the caustic vapours almost knocking me down cold feeling the heat shifting up and back, down my soft throat, feeling the accompanying warm glow. And the fire rising in my belly back then and in every single vein and beat of my heart and thought.

Come on we've got to go. Standing concentrating on the sounds of music demons licking their lips and sneering see you around and hissing. Sitting in the car feeling so alive. As if for the first time every breath a rebirth alive ecstatic euphoric better than making love some say. Name your poison and this can be better. Much better. The feelings so strong almost coming from the outside. Yeah. And again yes. Just so yes. Concentrating on the inside the nerve endings frying and recrystallising over and over with each throb sponging it up and sucking it out.

He walks into the newsagents. Stares and sways slightly. Too much time without the filling substances.

"Ten Marlborough please", spoken evenly with no emotion. Staring down into the palm of his hands where a few coins sit waiting for the exchange.

"Fifty-five pence please", she tries to look interested but inside she is secretly hating.

Soaking and bathing my shattered nerve ends over with each pulse flickering joy. The car speeding noiselessly down country roads back from Kettering. Town of horse thieves and demons. The trees cold hedges hot fences pulse real air. Throb. Real life. Beat. Place to get lost. Pulse place to be found. Beat.

Again. Again. Again. More. More. More. Pulse. Beat. Step. Left . Right.

Choirs of angels heavenly voices soothing now it was Wagner and Valkyries stirring my soul to new heights then. New ecstasy feeling the power and the glory amen. Wanting it. For everandever praying it would last .

Out of the shop feeling the plastic film of the packet snug in his hand in the pocket.

I'm having my day let me be. New York's streets paved with pus glowing with the scum of a newfound empire ready made. People dragged from the corners of the planet mother to us all. Money buys Monet and you all. Forget it. Right now just forget it. What I really want money just cant buy. Not from you ever. Like a dry tree seeking water. Thirsting for just one drop to sustain throughout the heat. Seems amazing how far we go just to survive what we'll do. If I had it you'd be first to be watered. This hand may want to squeeze away the life of the babe but I would feed you. Cool clear water icecold in the desert heat as you hold on hoping to get through this dry season this arid squalid plain of glass sand. Snaking sand eyes you impassively biding his time. He's got forever knowing he'll win it out in the end Methuselah. And yet you stand in the way continuing to haunt, and thwart him year by year. Two centuries of foxes the insects secure beneath your bark the sap rising through your veins and shaggy trunk the bird in the nest in your outstretched palm fist branch. They don't know how to worship yet they do. Even the small prairie dog lying in the shade cast by your mass pays homage whilst whispering to the sand.

Feeling every beat of my heart. Feeling the blood rushing and coursing my veins. Every beat an explosion sending out shockwaves from the centre of my soul , placed firmly in the pulsing orb in my chest , to extremities of mind and body. My hand clenched, the muscles along my forearm tightening then relaxed pumping the rivers of gushing blood faster and faster. My very fingertips burnt and froze as the feelings and sensations swelled and heaved as the sea lashing the pebbled shore . The tide relentlessly crashing . Wave upon wave never letting up . The blood. Coursing my veins and arteries seeking to burst every vessel with its sheer size and capacity .

Understood then. The meaning. Some sense of. Dunno . Just seemed a little better somehow. Existents. Existence. Between the waves in the lulls there. That's it. Between things. Events. Glistening shallow thoughts filled with existents. Existentless thoughts are pure .

This is what makes us alive. Muscles bones tendons each and every hair cell upon cell a single quivering universe shattering and coming to a new end and born dying again . Body shaking shattered no good . The electrons about each atom span faster .

Spiral twists of DNA making love falling through the endless black of that cosmos eclipsed by the heaving twisting spiralling strands of life never created ever destroyed. In their eternal dark lifeless universe of two lovers alone fluttering through infinity.

Whitehot swelling on fire and flying.

Divinity was now justified, anything was possible mountains could be moved seas could be parted.

He squats down outside the shop, lights a cigarette and stares across the street at the redbricked buildings.

Cars moving. Pedestrians making their way to work in the early morning.

Work. Jobs. Smiling again.

Sweet faced the smoke drew him in, the spider settling down to pray Buddha-like away above in the cold.

This was how it felt . At the dawn of creation . That quiet hum that filled the pure air the paradise san-Eden no cars planes houses telephones TVs radios people . The earth spinning more slowly and through the unbroken silence the hum of the friction caused by the new air grating against the alien mass of earth . An huge planet spinning and trying to speed up . To catch up with the others . Caliban morpheous zeo exxxon jupiter tempestuous brothers and sisters in the heavens . Falling out into space returning through the dark to the beginning .

May I return ? No . Its too late .

A planet lurching uneasily through its arcing circle . Nowhere else to go nothing else to do . The hum filling all nothing surviving it but the flora . Nothing slithered or crawled moving life was waiting for the glorious hum to finish . As that note faded the earth was unborn and ridden with our disease . Trees and grass watching silent in the green . To have been there watching the first golden sunrise the wonder of it all water against our naked flesh .

You with me together for the very first time . My sadness and lost . Our nakedness many caresses in the colden water pure fresh . We are so close the heat between us .

Just love.

Loving together with you feeling the pain of the planet. Crying in the pain.

Taking a slowdive into more cool waters. Why is it you always want the one thing we can't have.

The peace was gone, the darkness closing in, the overdose casting us down into Danteic depths of furious torment a sea of pain populated with devils snaking on their stomachs.

Misery hammering against my temples, ecstatic life replaced
with the chilliness of the void stepping from the car. Vomit
falling from lips tumbling down over my shoes. Reaching down
again to the very heart of my soul. Heart and soul devoured by
the white poison. Lights dancing before my eyes swirling in my
head, filled with pain. Oh crucifixion burning. Pathetic wretch
bile dribbles from that soft mouth as I am filled with pus.
Swimming as I gulp, drowning for air. Ignorance is my bliss.
Sinner by my own compulsions saving the hand that bites me. I
had blacked out still vomiting .

advert – Marlboro

de

con

stru

cti

on

As he sat there in the slight breeze, looking away to the farness
all those painful memories come and went. Flooded in, beautiful
young ladies and lovers so different and yet, the sameness. Hard
taught bodies. Sweet smelling wave falling cascading hair.

Love my way is a new romance. We knew it would be fatal to touch my lost encounter in a haze. Too much drink Dutch courage. But I know you will. Well. Would have felt. The current passed between us our eyes sparked. You looked sometimes as if you longed for me to hold you. But I didn't. Afraid.

I

Don't

Trust

myself.

Let us go then you and I . And I haunt your thoughts don't I? . The spiritwalker . A product of something so close . We could have made love that afternoon . Yet now I walk in your dreams . We were joined torn apart and reborn bonded . An eternal love affair that never ends . Silent only parted in unreality . We walk as one . Walked as two . And die every day together . Nobody comes between that . Jesus . I feel your loss and my pain longing to consume you to feel our love made real locked in embrace the love passing across flesh and here .

Firewhiteheatmelting as we fall into secrecy your cool hands tracing the ridges of my broken scarred flesh feeling the grooves and broken tissue .

A tender kiss . .Just one .

He pulled the old coat in tighter, drawing in any warmth that he could.

Proud pound .

The signs in the windows never change, Bradlaugh's statue stands pointing fingerless, the grass around its base withered in the heat of the previous two weeks the bare soil showing through. A pigeon standing thoughtfully on the head on this iconoclast, the sun starting to show its head above the gothic ornaments of the furniture showroom.

Beautiful sky . Cold up there Icarus golden cold almost Italian in blue dome . Feeling it up there .

Falling would be best .

He stood creaking up, ambled toward the town passing the clothes shop the alley and the art shop and the Racehorse public house all wood and glass and old.

Heels clicking on the paves, cold and fresh, for once the buckles jingling upon his boots with every footfall crossing the wide quiet road.

His thoughts wandered aimlessly and without thought and form, now in front of Bruger's jewellery shop next to the abandoned decay of an old Indian takeaway. In the shade the shadow of the unsun passing the corner going down York Road and again in the light, full dawn of the sun. Across again and through the alleyway into his glorious golden graveyard where so many things had happened. A squirrel scampered the graves, looking for buried treasure, grey pigeons roosted in the trees and the alcoves in the stained-glass windows. The path bisected and quartered the grounds of the dead, a sin to drink and smoke and laugh there, yet a place of great joy bliss and beautiful silence and finality.

The sunlight dappled him now, through the roof of elders he passed and out into the bright. Down the street to the park, the green grass stretching away down to the river and lagoon. He sits now on the slightly damp grass and pulls out his notebook and reads a short story. He smiles at the title "The Butterfly" an early expressive piece. Searching for his form and rhythm and style.

Love me now or break my back . Silk, against my hot flesh. The caress of your hidden hands. Our lips brush your cool body mine the heat and the tension building. I'm wound up like a spring a coil. Tighter and tighter we go higher and lower falling down into chaos theory. Hotter and hotter into and through exploding stars and supernovae.

I want to hold onto you forever.

Then its over.

> *Tiger, tiger burning bright*
> *In the forest in the night,*
> *From deep within my soul there shines*
> *A red psychotic light.*

He lies on the cool wet early morning grass of the park; there was little to disturb the air with sounds here, excepting the birdsong. The lighter was still in his pocket, he could still feel its warm rectangular pleasing heaviness, feel the pockmarked ridged surface in the fingers of his right hand - but then it was gone - he hadn't found it yet.

I wasn't sure if you were dying. Smells and sounds of the nursing home. All running as normal while you were dying. The breath from your chest rattling its way out. Cracking and popping sounds they call it. The nurse changes the bed linen from your room mates bed. Lying now like a baby. Reverting back you lay there. The day before it was touch and go. How long does it take to die?

Fiercely holding onto your life. The most precious gift ever given. Been in a vegetative state for three years. Almost no humanity left. Extreme advanced dementia. Frontal lobe of your brain almost gone. Eaten away. Almost none of your memories intact now. First few months you held onto your cherished memories but somehow erasing unwanted or unknown pleasures. But then the scarring and the disease has eaten them all away. Your brain being picked clean, a carcass covered in flies and maggots.

Heh. Like that old photo of Hiroshima with just that one building left standing. An observatory? Was it?

You're sleeping peacefully now. Then. Then. So surprised this happened. Not expecting it. You just went down. Bang. Into hospital and then this. Where did it come from?

Sleeping like a baby. Like a baby now. In my mind's eye you are there curled up like a foetus.

The day before you were all agitation. Your eyes and hands moving, doing something.

Your hands moving in agitation trying to repeat some operation they had carried out in the past. Like reflex reaction. Like a lizards tail after its been cut off still reacting but with no conscious control. No control. Hand clawing at the air in agitation. Something you did in the past? Some repetitive action that has stayed inside your brain all these years to come out now in a kind of final release. A burst of something. Some electrical signals passing somewhere. Some synapses closing or opening sending a message. Or is it the muscles spasming erratically? Almost like playing charades, your twisted hands gripping and clenched tight shut. Have been for months. What are you doing?

In your mind so many fantasies replacing reality. And you forgot mum. You forgot. Maybe it's a kind of kindness? Like the antechamber of death. A waiting room. Waiting for a space? Surely heaven doesn't have a maximum capacity? Or hell? Or. Oh wait that's where the zombies come from. Ouch. Zombies. Not thinking of them there then.

He turns his head. Just lying in the sun. Listening to the sounds and the breath of the wind gentle over his reclining figure. Drifting in and out of reverie. Memory to memory. This one focused and powerful. As it had been happening he had sat there. Watching taking it all in.

Making notes in my small note book. Recording sounds. Noting everything. Recording the actuality of what its like. Seeing father slip into death. Not exactly comfortably but... had to record that. Had to record it. Sit impassively with my notebook scribbling away. So that these memories that flashed across my mind could now be so much more real than imagined writings of death.

The sky is such a beautiful azure blue deep blue. The small white fluffy clouds move across slowly. So white but tipped with greys and mauves and purples and small light violets. Insects humming in the air. The steady gentle murmur of traffic in the background. Soft wet morning dew, Lying on a slope. The grass gently sloping down to the lagoon and the river. His favourite place.

My lonely place. Place where I go alone and would one day love to take my children.

After this death to come.

A preparation then for the change of perspective from life to death. Your asleep now. In that foetal position. Clutching the thin sheets to your chest and tummy. Holding them close to you. Lying so still but your knuckles white grasping these thin sheets.

*You are tiny now, weight like five stone? Arms and legs so thin.
Look like an Auschwitz victim. And the bruising of old age.
Bruises come up big and black and black red ambering to the
edges mottled. Never realised. Bruise so easily now the skin is so
thin and taught over wasted muscles and tendons. Like nothing I
ever seen. Looking like a sparrow.*

*The vacant stare now and then. Pretty vacant. Really nothing
there. No recognition of me. No recognition of where or when or
who. Or when. Time drifting.*

His eyelids are closed.

*We can step through the memories and back to that time. We all
can. Just that we are too scared to do so.*

*I looked at the pillows. The soft warm pillows. I really nearly did
it. Looking and then wondering who made me god? Taking a
life. Even this frankly worthless life wasn't my decision to make.
Ending the suffering? Still not sure. This must surely be the most
important question ever. By a long way. To take away a life?
For whatever reason? How?*

He continues to lie on the grass, staring at the blue sky, the soft
clouds continue to scud across gently. It is such a beautiful day.
The sky really is so blue. The sky really is so high and so far
away. Colours are so hard to understand or to explain to those
who have never seen them.

If you made a thinking machine would it ever learn colour? Understand colour? Can you understand colour without emotion to translate it? Could you build a machine and add emotion? Science fiction.

You're there hands like talons more animal than human. Like a bird's foot all twisted up with unbearable tension. Radio on. Playing Duran Duran. Conversations drifting around the nursing home. Occasionally a scream. A shout. Like an old home for the insane. A modern day mad-dog ward. So many faces staring blankly. No conversation left. No life left in them. They should make children see this. Our old need compassion too. They need our love most of all. At least I tried to give you what love I could Dad. I did my best. Can't do more than that.

Banging your clenched fist against the metal rails of the bed frame. Like a prisoner trying to break free. Bang. Bang. Bang. Staring into space. Looking a million miles away. Are you calling? Your mouth moving silently not enough breath to push a word out or a sentence. Are you calling out to your mother? Rattling the bed. Why? Over and over again I think why?

Then you stop breathing and your eyes glass over unseeing. And I reach out to you. Leaning over. Thinking your dead.

Constant noise in the background. Is this your dignity? Is this degrading. Mine. Mine. Mine you seem to be saying. What's yours Dad? Then you go silent. Breathing heavy and laboured now like a child with a fever you're thrashing around a little. What little strength you have left in your brittle bones and tendons and emaciated muscles. Coughing and gurgling from somewhere deep down inside you. Your wedding ring banging against the metal of the bed frame. And my only way to cope is to sit there and write it all down.

Death bed. So this is what it means. This is a death bed waiting.

White wall beside your head so cold and inviting to you. To something inside you. It is stained and marked with finger marks. Finger prints. Smudged dirty marks where your hand has palmed it. Where your fingers have tried to grasp it and feel it to see if it is still real.

The smell of piss and shit fills the air.

Rubbing your hands together and occasionally clawing at the sheet finding some strength from somewhere.

Then its all quiet again.

He takes out a cigarette and sits up cross legged like a Buddha. Lights the cigarette and inhales deeply.

Smoke giving me life. Not taking it away. The drift in time now back to then again. Exhale.

Mouth is hanging open now. And this is how you will look right at the end and that is what we will never forget. That look when there is an absence of life. But not yet. Teeth yellow. Now your trying to write in the air with your clawed up talon. Your trying to sit up. I look at you impassively like an observer. A watchman.

And then its days later and your almost still. Almost completely unmoving. Last rattles of breath from your chest. Low moans. Gentle agitation. Eyes long since able to see and a brain long since able to function. Gently spasming again. Unconscious reactions? No feeling? Murmuring gently saying the same thing again over and over. Words not fully formed I lean over to try and catch them and make sense of them. Your still hearing me and responding to touch occasionally. Like a blind man.

I watch your diaphragm moving slowly up and down waiting for it to stop. You are fighting so hard to save something, what is it? The most precious gift the universe can bestow which we spend most of our lives ignoring. Like a codex we should read and never do. Distracting ourselves into day-to-day bullshit.

Only here on this death bed does it really show how rare and wondrous this thing called life really is. This tiny spark. This golden spark we carry around in our hearts

Tiny golden multicoloured spark we carry around in an endless sea of oblivion and entropy.

Then you aren't there anymore and that's it. Mouth hangs open half-closed eyes stare, glassed over, no focus.

And its over.

The cigarette is finished now and he looks calm. He stands easily and walks slowly across the morning dewy grass. Walks slowly down to the river where the old bridge crosses the slowly flowing weeded waters beneath. He steps onto the wood feeling its safety rising through his boots. He crosses the bridge, looking over the edge into the deep slow flowing waters and reeds and at the ducks and geese and other living things dwelling there. In front of him now there is a raised lagoon with a small island in its centre. This was a peaceful place, Irises grew in the shallow water around, and birds settled both on the island and in the trees surrounding the lagoon.

He walks to the right, passing the weir and the boathouse and a particularly fine Willow stopping now and then to look into the sun dappled water, as flies buzz and insects skate the smooth surface of the gently undulating water. Having completed three-quarters of the circuit he stops and sits down on an old concrete bench by the water's edge.

He lights another a cigarette using a booklet of matches from an American motel. The cardboard matches have bright orange tips, and spark and flare briefly, glowing red then dying with a puff of grey black smoke. He rolls the match between his fingers and flicks it with a tiny hiss into the lake. The gentle wind carries the match far out into the lake.

Thirty-seven thousand years and we've come to this.
Civilization.

He lays back in the warming sun, closing his eyes as he exhales the smoke quickly drifting away.

Not afraid anymore. But I remember when I was young.

That night was black, not a normal black, but a total darkness that was new and frightening as I lay in half-sleep, just drifting and floating here and there. Slept in many beds and on many floors, many times but here it was different no streetlights, no cars. Just total darkness which nuzzled softly at the window pane trying to get in.

Lying there in bed it seems there is no difference between us. I can feel the peace and calm . The darkness pulsating around us . You and I . As we slept together in the womb . Outside I could hear the wind racing across the tips of the corns in the field, hear the waves beating the shore and the fisher-kings far out at sea , their boat rising on the swell as they let out their nets .

Two men were talking . The older one struck a match , it flared a flash-light photograph etched on my memory of that dark lined face as it sucked and puffed on that old pipe , laughed and joked with the young helper . A boy barely seventeen sitting adoring at the elder's feet .

The water was cool as I broke its solid surface and felt the air rushing away . The waters blackness was intense , but it was not this which scared me . It was the huge dark shapes moving with great power and majesty through the deep, deeper I sank . Past these great lumbering giants , brushing slightly against them drinking in their mass strength and solidity . The huge warm eyes looked at me once then turned away with contempt .

I sank until I floated in nothing, passed through to somewhere else. I opened my mouth to question the greenblack dark but the sea washed into my lungs, filling them with small eyeless albino fish, weeds and burning salt water.

The old man in the boat stopped laughing and told the young lad to quickly pull in the nets .

The young one jumped at the order , machinery jolted into life the clanking noises boomed and pumped through the waters darkness as the large shapes moved closer for an instant dwarfing me.

I unable to make out specifics can only see huge darkness and huge slightly lightness against the endless black velvet of the Loch. Still deep dark waters, weeds down there at the bottom so far away but tendrils clutching upwards trying to draw down the breathing and throttle them into watery death.

The huge monsters then left me alone moving silently as beasts in their kingdom of grace .

The nets heaved the slack was taken up and quickly chased onto the spindle .

As I arose from my sunken tomb I could see two white faces stark against the dark starry sky both concerned peering down into the water . I gasped as I broke surface and the fresh air filled my lungs , the oxygen flooding the tiny veins shattering my frozen heart back into life

The old man knocked his pipe on the side of the boat as he picked me up crossing himself with whispered prayers in Latin . Looking upon my blackness. The darkness of this heart and the blood from my gaping lungs black and cold. He tossed me one-handed high into the air, following my arc with his eyes, upwards ever higher , my tail and fins swimming through the air.

Higher I swam .

The small white farmhouse with its tin roof on the side of the hill, the town five miles away , all were below . Higher still the emerald isle was clear , till the clouds obscured the view . Onwards and upwards standing floating on the edge looking down . Its somewhere you just have to be . To see the arc of the Earth, to see its blue. The real blue. The white of the clouds and that curve. To see the golden glimpsing moment when the sun appears like the greatest magic trick ever seen. Blasting its fiery rays into your eyes. Not protected by atmosphere out here. Up here in the calm empty airless void. Down again the earth trying to suck me down there. The earth span slowly unstopping the sun rising fast to my left and the world brighten in the morning glow of dawn . Her golden rays blinded me as she appeared in the rarefied cold clean air from the void .

I could look no more . See no more . Through the clouds I saw the earth's beauty a wholeness suspended , filling everything a beautiful blue green swirl flecked with white .

She fills your sight no matter how hard you look up down left right she is everything. She is our home our lover our protector our mistress our lover our own dark end sucking our remains into her womb to care for them forever.

No entropy. Evolution. Atoms expanding and contracting.
Endless recycling and peace interrupted by this oh so beautiful
time in this Garden of Eden which somehow we have forgotten is
our only home. Home to such diversity. I drill my mind down
into the seas and marvel at the single celled amorphous lives
swimming glowing neon-light in the blackness.

I saw her and cried .

My faith no more I fall back , cradled in gravity's palm sucked
down through the rushing light .

Spinning spinning as I fall backward somersaults again in the
foetal position , wailing , my stomach a blackhole sucking me in
, round and round , spinning my screams cutting the air's flesh ,
through the dark womb of the planet . The silence pressed
against me , this was black and white , no colours , moving
falling spinning somersaulting hurtling faster and
faster , silently my hands clasped tightly about my head covering
eyes and ears .

It stopped .

Rushing screams shrill and piercing filled my mind screams and
blasting pressure the air ripped again into vacant lungs filling .

Ten thousand feet above Manhattan , falling , my eyes centred on the streets , glowing gold with the money of another day of trading , far below , the golden glow too , on the clouds fluffing as sheep .

Down I fell , twixt the two great fingers reaching up from the bedrock toward the weightless blue , dreamy twisted skyscrapers in defiance . I tried to fly , flapping comically like a man running toward the pavement , not like a doll , vacant and unpleasing , but a struggling life soul sprinting at terminal velocity .

Suddenly we are in a slowmotion event. Life moves on now frame-by-frame slowly agonisingly slowly inches from the sidewalk. I can smell the dew on the dust and grime and dirt feel the roots of life somewhere far below , the consciousness of the place and the planet lost forever now .

A cockroach is scuttling across the slab feet moving so beautifully slowly . I study the fine hairs and strength of its shell and eyes as they finally perceive me and the look of barren wonder and , astonishment as my face is pushed up into my brain .

For an instant we two are one again.

The sun's light is so warm, intense, a rosy shine on his face. A fly hums over the still of the murky lagoon. Monotonous tone of wasps and bees and flying insects buzzing suspended in the warming air, part of a chain of competing catalysts vying for air supremacy. A partly quiet untroubled existant lay swaddled in an old coat black and dark , long tousled hair blonde from a bottle , gothic boots with tight black faded to grey shiny jeans . The dragon-fly hovers like an attack helicopter inches from his face, a meta-insect devourer of the smaller, perfect attack vehicle.

Man takes thirty-five thousand years to build an ornithopter which still cannot match this grace created from nature's beauty and scalpel.

Nature being a doctor, or more rightly a chirugeon, picking the meat from the bones and fatty tissue. The weak cut away like a cancer falling beneath the surgeons delicate bladed fingers. Dream on, mankind; hope for an answer but instantly dismiss any proposals.

This miniature helicopter contains it, floating in the warm breath of another kind of flyer, a dreamer of cornucopical bliss . Elegant splendour of Byronic hedonism encapsulated in this still small voice in there, in the head, in the brain - thinking not of words, but pictures and photos a competing chain of signifiers never connecting like links in at train track but like the strands and branches and leaves of a tree.

Society is a carnivorous flower. Potentially beautiful. Soft. Fragrant and inviting. Welcoming and accepting. Fragile and multicoloured and soft-textured. Pinks and blues and purples. And gold. Soft green leaves succulent. But still a dangerous and murderous intent lurks there inside. Simple snares. Traps. A tiny money spider slowly crawls up the stem. Entranced. A gentle eight-legged ballet. Tiny steps. Up and up. One by one. Leg by leg. Many eyed spider. The flower waiting to devour it. Not thinking. No brain to think.

This flower a mixture of beauty and cruelty. A rhythm of cruelty.

I really have got to admire your ingenuity.

Our society wanted us to conform. To behave. To fall into its compliance. How does society deal with us outsiders? How did it deal with us? Dirty punks. Those who wouldn't fit in? The flowers in the dustbin spreading wild poison into the human part of the machine. And at all levels the poison fed on the compliant parts of the machine. Always and forever the cogs and the wheels gagged when trying to compile another misfit. Another part of the machine would have to labouriously start itself back up into life. Its reincarnated corpse dripping with the sweat, blood and secretions of those it had crushed.

As soon as one of the fat pig Judges began to dig deeper into a case and look at the protests and the evidence it was terminated with extreme prejudice. Yeah. And that Judge was then cut apart from the body, the society, and another was grown in its place. The offending Judge was ex-communicated. The new Judge more compliant in its thinking. A part of the God-fearing poisoned machine worshipping greed and uniformity than that Judge which had been rejected for its compassion.

The Klan. Is the Police. Is the Mafia.

Over and over again.

He lies in the warm summer air. The sounds of insects gently humming in the still morning air. The traffic a dull and gentle murmur moving about its daily business. Carrying its people to God-knows-where for God-knows-what reason. Commerce.

State control. My own tacit consent of its existence and its power over me. My inability to fully reject it and follow my own ideals. Never full able to embrace the alternative. Living on the edge of those who did rather than considered. Animal rights activists who were prepared to stand and fight for their beliefs. To give up their freedom to end the suffering of our dumb partners on this beautiful swirling blue planet filled with wonders. Respect to those who were trying, seeking to find a way to infiltrate and eradicate the society which threatened to kill us all. Really I'm just too damn scared of authority.

His long hair is blown about casually by the gentle wind which also carries the odd snatch of a conversation to him. His chest rising and falling as the air rushes in and out. He is thinking.

Walking. Walking. So much walking. Miles. Just like Nanny. She walked. Walked to look for a clue to her past in Dublin. To find a place she could remember. But she never did.

And I walk?

And keep walking.

Not standing still. You cant stand still.

If you do you stop breathing. Walking up to Clifford Mill Hill. Up the hill. Into the old warehouse there. Sometimes exploring the old boot and shoe warehouses which were being torn down one by one.

It wasn't so long ago that you could walk past Waukerz Boot factory and see all the men outside on their break. Drinking their tea [milk and three sugars] in the late morning sunshine. Lined faces, but carefree. Smiling and joking. Some had their eyes closed just drinking in the fresh morning air and the warm summer sun. The golden rays and the gentle breeze. Twenty minutes then back inside to get on with the Important business of making boots fit for royalty.

Most of these factories were now little more than empty shells. The machines, human or otherwise, long since gone. Dead. Retired. Decommissioned. No one needed their smiles and skills any longer. All boots and shoes made by automatons, robots. No hand-stitched uppers. Man made – but not by man. By mindless machines. Unthinking slaves following their programming and their code.

Walking across London. The dark metropolis. Late at night. Head down sometimes. Looking inconspicuous. Other times head held high. Long hair flowing out behind. Looking up sometimes at the tall dark and lonely empty buildings. The chill winds of London biting me. Robbing me of any heat and the growing hunger inside me. Not able to eat. No money. Destitute and wandering the streets. Looking and watching. Sometimes stood stock still or squatting down in a doorway. Huddled inside my long black overcoat to light a cigarette. As evening falls around us.

Fags made from dog-ends. As usual. Found on the ground near telephone boxes. Repeating myself again. Stained cigarettes but still that rush of sweeet nicotine hitting the back of my head. The hot smoke filling my lungs and making me whole again. For a short time. Memories. Of fading light. The cold white stark moon hanging in the sky over Tower Bridge. The long and lonely walk back across London to Euston. And back to here. And back to now.

Which was then

To that home. So empty now. Silent and brooding. All broken and torn.

Happier times. Yes. Slip into them. Fall into that hot warm bath and imagine the water washing away my violence and my sins. Pick one out and hold it in my mind. In this thing which makes me do my living. Like eat and breathe and sleep and love and live. Brain. Centre of? Heart and soul? Thought is king. Heart feels. Stomach feels sometimes. Heart loves? Heart is empty and cold. Mind is part of brain? Thinks.

It's a complicated jigsaw. Pieces which fall together. Like DaDa. Random. Random? Seeking order. From the falling pieces of paper. So where? Happier times. Trying to drag myself into one of them.

Time's come and time's yet to go or yet to be. Still over the horizon. One by one. Day by day. Instant by instant. One after another cascading down life's waterfall. Flaming alloys. Free flowing instants moving. Becoming. And then gone.

Try again to capture and hold those happier times. A happy time. A good day to die. Or to remember. Sweet caresses and loving tender embrace. Sensual touch. Silk against my flesh. To put that longing away.

But here and now in this glorious sun. In the summertime of my late youth trying to imagine what it will be like to be old. To be thirty. No forty. No. Dead. Too much. Going too far. Burning up in this summer sun heat. I am here now and I do exist now and I am real now. More real than words. You read this and are here with me now. Forever now. Forever here and feeling what I feel. Like in a novel. Or a film. Reading this passage back over and over again. The endless scenes replaying as the flowers are washed away by the rain. Stood by the gate at the foot of the garden. Caressed by a beauty that burns from inside.

See?

So hard to think and make these thoughts into real words which make sense. My words come and go. More often than not. Sometimes struggling to find the correct word to fit the picture. Wonder what the stranger wants? Him all dressed in black. Watching. Been doing it for some time now. Weeks on and off. Months maybe before I noticed him.

And the messages coming to me from the news on TV. The voices calling me and whispering to me in the moments of quiet. Today so quiet. This one day alone. Like Dedalus. Wandering my own Odyssey. And still trying to. Pin. Down. That. One. Happy. Memory.

There are so many.

A single flower in the desert. Aylesbury Civic Arena. Awash with the debris of society. Youths. Pink hair. Red hair. Black hair. Dreadlocks. Mohicans. Shaved heads. Piercings and tattoos. Punks. Positive punks we/they were called. All waiting and watching. Nervous excited smiles. The air filled with the glory of electricity and tension and aggression. Electric atomic expectation. We all stared at the stage together. A coming together.

The lights dimming. The backdrops. A slight hum from the PA and then it all goes dark and the hush really does fall over the crowd. A few whispered voices. The odd laugh. The bodies of the tribe are preparing themselves. Some turn and look around them seeking something. Looking for old faces and old friends. There are no battery humans here. I inhale. Breathe this in. The mix of sweat. Patchouli. Hashish. Alcohol. Perfume. Mostly a male dominated dancing space. Some of the older, seasoned punks gather at the front. Centre stage.

And now the ominous operatic music swells. That old tune from the Old Spice adverts. Carmen Burina or something. Never did bother to find out what it was called. Never cared enough. I just knew it meant they were coming. And there I stood rooted to the spot. Eyes wide. Speeding out of my head. Heart pumping. Waiting. Looking to the stage. Fidgeting. Leg twitching.

Then the crowd roar. And truly a Southern Death Cult walk onto the stage into the light. Alive with raw energy. A tribal trance. A ceremony. And did we worship? I think I did. I think I drank it all in. Standing there. Absorbing the moment. Were we all worshippers? Or is that just too romantic?

This was the New Church. This was the New Cathedral of Punk. Out of the rotting and stagnant corpse of 1977 the new naughty children were playing their new punk rock music. And we danced. Oh how we danced. And whirled. Like dervishes truly. Not an exaggeration to say we heaved and pulsed and writhed en masse. One giant human machine. We strutted. Yes like peacocks. Yes it's a cliché.

And we all suddenly somehow believed it was all going to be ok.

And here in front of us was a man with a vision. And he was so filled with his hate and pent up aggression. He moved like a dancer across the stage.

Face painted in his tribal colours and markings. Half red. Half white? Not sure I remember. Not much but his burning eyes. He was the new Jim Morrison. A new Johnny Lydon? No. So much more than that.

The sneer on his lips at times. Leading us in a new Lord's Prayer. We swayed and we sang along. Chanted. We danced and we held onto something. This church was filled with acolytes. And we danced. Sweat dripping from my body. My t-shirt drenched. Soaked. Sweat and heat. Leather jackets. Studs. Did we all pray at this ceremony looking for new gods? I was certainly swept away as the music washed over me. Rising and lifting guitars. Brooding thundering bass. Tribal pounding drums. So sweet. Such sweet communion. Sinking and falling into a kind of bliss at that moment. That singular moment in time. My time in my memory. So far away now.

The hovering floating killer dragonfly moved away.

Drum pattern thrusts and peaks thudding. Never anything to do in this town. They're right, totally. God. We will stare and stare across the eons you and me. At each of our selves in multiplicity eyes bleeding tears warm of blood. Haunted over these years yet to pass. Transubstantiation. We could choose words like lies. Snapshots. Memories. I will set you on fire.

"Look, you've got to seek sense, it won't just appear like some fucking ghost… it's there if you'll look hard enough… but you just don't try do you? Eh? Do you? We can't go on like…"

The voice mocks him and teases his senses.

The stranger stands and watches still. All dressed in black.

And then we died.

This was not the sort of death we read about in novels, this is real death. Death like you're scared of, the big one your very own private personal trail over the edge, pain and fear, that one which creeps closer and closer every day, hour minute second. I can talk here quite impassively since I have been dead many centuries now. It slid up over our face blocking eyes, flowing gently into mouth filling it, our nose too. It takes a year at least, and never stops or slows, you can't take anymore but it keeps oozing and sucking lurching like the tides of lava from Vesuvius, or the tar which trapped a mammoth and held it suspended for millennia until today.

Can you taste it? No.

They keep on laughing and eating whilst you exorcise a lifetime's dreams and memories, dying in your own private ecstasy.

Finally two icy fingers push into your ears, searching and slipping, probing grasping at your mind. Tickling the edges at first with a spasm of sexual energy. A jerkoff release from your temporal idolatory of now. As you relax from your exertions a hand now forces entry into your mouth gagging your voice and those endless screams and wails bemoaning and cursing with prayer.

A cold freezing hand pushes brutally down into you, squeezing and pulling at heart beating fitfully, almost powerfully in a last outburst of faith and belief, a sneer at creation. And God. In its last gasp, it is crushed. The hand tugs and tears, it freed rises through the destroyed flesh and spirit. That sinking feeling. Still warm beating life, detached ex-spiriti sancti , searing cold , finally extracting from your mouth the last remnants of life of humanity . Black dark blood, now cold, fills the void of red, that unbelievable space, a gaping sucking wound, tasting the sweet juice as your face bewears the idiot's leer, a drool.

You think of lost lovers the ones we will never meet and feel cheated. Its another sad affair. Lovers come and go, this is been carried around by me forever, they never stay to the end. Love lies, all the things I never did.

Mother. father. Lost chances lost futures. An end to all the beginnings the final journey.

Slipping and sliding down into the endless pit of nothing. Falling falling . Like a star imploding. Impossible to understand to comprehend as the synapses meld into one last outburst. Just emotion left. No thought. No feeling. Just a sense of unbeing. Disconnected from. Not a part of. No senses. No sight. No sounds. Last thing to go are the sounds of the cool early morning air. The insects buzzing and the water running. The gentle sound of the breeze. Lulling calming. A simple ray of light unthinking.

Perspective is changing dancing brain trying to hold onto itself.
Its belief . No body ever taught us how to do this. A one-off
experience.

We are sacred scared inhuman inhumane excorporate other
black light unholy unwhole diswhole exwhole folded in on
ourself shrinking ever in at odds with physicality and reason.

Until we are simply.

No.

It surrounds and is everything, everywhere.

It is complete in vacuous fullness, darker than black. So much
darker than black. As my thoughts float unbodied in a starless
loveless multi-dimension, dis-universal in-finite nothing.

No. Love no. Feeling without . No light air just draughts of inky
seasaltywater . Alone.

This is real.

In unreality. No heaven? No hell?

These are not even questions anymore. The wonder is the experience of experiencing the nothingness which our heads now have to quantify and deal with . You can't. Its just knowing, no feeling, absence of everything corporeal and physical.

What he wanted to protect us from. The inhumanity of real life. Extended universal existence. Formless with no points of reference. Too much for us. Death is so real in superreality it exists in temporal terms so big in its hideous loneliness. Like talking with a star or a blade of grass.

All I have left are the bladed memories of another time so different. A fiction, loaded with form and state.

Jigsaw memory shifts and realigns adjusting its self to this impossible unreality. To cry would be a blessing, a single tear, but there is no room here.
Only empty lost souls shattered in their exile of excessive non-relativity. Loveless dying souls that cannot quite let their consciousness slip forever, flatlining brains tumble from our unhappy non-gathering splendid isolation, perfect dissymmetry.

To what am I attached, what holds me back up pushes and turns me? Humanity? Futures seen and never tasted? Revenge? is this a dream or the actual reality following the discomfortable physicality of the flesh we walk around in for four-score years and ten?

Life seems so precious. You fight hard to hold onto it.

You will. Believe me you wont achieve a letting go for eons, even here in the face of this hideous strength. But eventually we all do, dismantling moment by moment the component memories of a lifetime beyond comprehension now.

It is the final unspeakable journey. The defining moment of whitehot joy and gutwrenching pain all rolled into one. Without any doubt the one thing we will never understand. What we are all born to experience and what none of us ever can comprehend. The splitting and shattering of a billion memories. Energy not created nor destroyed. Transmuted in that dark unplace.

Having time [?] and depth [?] and distance [?] and form [?]

Finally pulling the fibres of conscious existence asunder wrenching them into a nothing as our flesh and limbs muscle rot and split in our wooden coffincages.

Is death life pure and distilled primitive universal cosmos?

We never die, not fully, are transmuted, flesh becomes fodder becomes bacteria swarming microscopic in deity form over the microbes and atoms. A god in a drop of dew able to pass with all the riches of bacterial life through the eye of a needle. These germs have no consciousness, yet they are. And will always be. They don't need God as much as us. Yet they live. Existents.

A meaning. We all strive for this. Life so vague, so cloudy with doubleedged doubt we don't want lifted. I hear about karma and the devil but it all sounds the same but eternal in cycle. Maybe I was on that barren open plain a small wooden shack called home shielding a few bright flowers from the oncoming hurricane filled black air. I will search myself so hard ill find out.

One day.

Eon.

This writing however, was nothing but a name repeated in all kinds of characters.

Silence.

Silence.

Beat.

Silence.

Shot like a bullet into the light, so fast the friction glows and burns white, a swimming shooting blazing human torch, across the dark purple filament of a circular sky, extended ever out. There it goes again, now with hope. An embryo sicked up, puked kicking, and screaming another day. You've got it all; in his heart you wore the hair of dreams, a love.

This pain was so beautiful following the void. Feels movement but is unaware of time speed or destination cannot comprehend such things after the many lifetimes spent disconnecting from consciousness and this super reality. Voices scream the house down again. Alien floating symbols, jagged with form, incorporate life and weight. His hand stretches out to a dying star to seek question and gain audience, it recoils to the land of the dead, leaving the hero trapped and earthbound.

A truth we promised.

Time has been cheated - this he knows.
The blind fear death less than we have seen it and drunk deep of its vaporous still perfume since birth, embracing the loneliness the emptiness which for them is undeniably filled. They have been living with more than one foot in the grave since start of, though they perceive no darkness, no alternative to things, except feel smell taste and sound. Read no fear in the loss of senses they already understand.

Suddenly we hit the air and drop like a brick into a body, corporate existent, and feel the blood bones and tissue of a body. So this is where I came from? This is how I was made? This is my birth.

Yes.

We've cheated death, and now I've cheated time, all that would have been is now gone.

"3484u nhuvg jv 3293u tb j t jei ji v,;ieg0=95945k f kdgiergirw '1"

"nfjnguty347ywe049i6ub oefkgokr rogkopeSoyi 462346"

"befhgbyweyr we4yjk possible kfn4S 485jgtr21=o"

"Fucking what?!"

The words made little sense, but the emotional impact was understood, belief horror joy. He expressed his own feelings, sending out a wave of relief, but this was not felt by his companions. Words spin, occasionally jump out and register a sense, a textual conclusion in his mind associated with the semiotics of picture language. Reason wrestles against this re-reality state - it cannot be.

A rushing wind is howling in his chest, accompanied by stretching muscle tissue and expansion, an alien breeze he wants to push away, too antiseptic. The light is a hideous burn, bright again blinding through filmy eyelids.

He screams and gulps too quickly, taking in lungfuls of air, too big straining the wasted muscles, ears filled with shouts, skin feels the burning tingling sway of the moving air about him. Shudder, whole body shudders as he tries to lift an arm, move a leg.

Scream againandagain, without sound, guttural throat gurgles as the sound is caught and trapped in the thick plastic tube. He gags twice trying to remove the obstruction, starts vomiting and choking as the thing is pulled wrenched out, he reaches down but something's not there, there is a dichotomy of action - straining muscles with an absence of the steadiness in life.

The reassuring thumpthump returns filling every space in his mind.

Feels, no, senses, the pain in his left arm and down his back across his legs and spine, pulling his heart down, that crushing weight.

Then a   **?**

The bluewhite clean jolt shocks his flesh burning and burrowing down shaking his insides. Rushing over his face and lips it hammers, ripping the cold hard lump into life, the valves open and fluid swims freely once again. The heart screeches and complains bitterly, rumbles quietly and rings with the resonant bassboom of life.

Thump

A beating a flooding.

Thump.

A gash a wish an hush of air.

Thump thump.

More pain, tears sting black eyes.

Thump.

Cold flesh his face, thump, cold crystal eyes.

Thump thump.

A gulp a gasp.

Drowning . Man.

He turns his head, neck muscles strain to scream.

Oh. My. Sweet. Lord.

And so after ten years deep in a coma he takes his first true breath. Truly the first breath under his own control. And so it was that he could hear, think, see and be human again.

He inhales deeply. Alive again. Back from the beyond. And back from the nothingness.

The dreams of reason do bring upon,
Such errors born of monsters,
Out of Madness

Made in the USA
Columbia, SC
12 January 2018